STOLEN STORMY NIGHTS

STEAMY PRIDE AND PREJUDICE VARIATION

DEMI MONDE

BELLA BREEN

BREEN PUBLISHING LLC

CHAPTER 1

In the quiet corner of Derbyshire, Elizabeth Bennet found herself in the enchanting company of her beloved aunt and uncle, the Gardiners. The sun shone brightly, casting a golden hue over the lush greenery that surrounded them. Bees buzzed around the colorful flowers, filling the air with their sweet fragrance, as the infectious laughter of old friends echoed through the countryside.

As they reclined in the elegant drawing room of their acquaintances' lavish home, the Gardiners exchanged fond memories, reminiscing about days gone by. Elizabeth listened intently to their animated conversation, her heart swelling with affection for her amiable relatives. She savored every moment, feeling grateful to be alive on such a beautiful day.

However, Elizabeth's adventurous spirit soon yearned for the thrill of exploration, and she politely excused herself from the gathering.

"I shall return shortly, Aunt," she assured Mrs. Gardiner. "I simply cannot resist the allure of the beautiful countryside."

Her aunt's knowing gaze followed her as she slipped out of the drawing-room door, no doubt aware of Elizabeth's restless nature.

Once outside, Elizabeth drew in a deep breath of the balmy air and stretched her limbs, reveling in her newfound freedom. Now, which hidden nook of the picturesque grounds would she discover today?

Her feet carried her down a winding garden path, past fragrant rose bushes, and a burbling brook. A gentle breeze rustled the leaves overhead, dappling the path with shadows. The sounds of her relatives' lively discourse faded into the distance behind her.

Before long, Elizabeth's wanderings led her to a small stone gazebo secluded behind a copse of trees. Her eyes widened in delight at the discovery, and she hastened her step. What a perfect secret sanctuary this would make for reading or reflection!

She settled onto a wooden bench within the gazebo, leaning her head back against the wall to take in the beauty of her surroundings. A deep sense of contentment stole over her as a lone songbird began to chirp merrily outside. The rustling leaves and babbling brook created a symphony of sound that soothed her soul. Truly, there were few pleasures so sweet as escaping into the beguiling Derbyshire countryside on such a fine summer's day. Elizabeth sighed, wishing she could stay in this idyllic moment forever.

But her curiosity got the best of her, and she decided to explore further. Beyond the gazebo, Elizabeth discovered a charming footpath that snaked through a dense grove of trees. She left the gazebo to follow the path, her heart pounding with excitement.

The dappled sunlight filtering through the canopy above cast an enchanting spell upon the scene, and Elizabeth felt her spirit soar with each step she took as though she were uncovering secrets hidden within the picturesque landscape. The crunch of twigs and the rustle of leaves beneath her feet added to the sense of adventure.

After some time ambling along in a contented reverie, Elizabeth emerged from the woods near a large pond. A flock of white geese drifted across the still water while a frog leaped with a splash from its leafy perch on the bank.

Elizabeth stood contemplating the idyllic view before her, breathing in the rich scent of moss and bracken that lingered in the air. As she continued to stroll along the charming footpath, she felt as if she were stepping into a painting or a dream. The cacophony of the geese and the faint rustling of leaves brought her back to reality, but the magic of the moment lingered on.

Lost in thought, Elizabeth scarcely noticed the path that led her to unfamiliar territory. The grove seemed never-ending, its dense foliage obscuring the view of the world beyond. As she wandered further, a sudden change in the atmosphere caught her attention. The once-warm sun vanished behind ominous clouds that rolled in from a distance. The gentle breeze grew into a forceful gale, the trees bending and swaying with its intensity. The sky darkened, casting eerie shadows upon the ground as a sense of foreboding settled over Elizabeth.

Realizing the imminent arrival of an unanticipated and powerful storm, Elizabeth's heart raced. She must find shelter before the rain began to fall, but it appeared she had chosen the wrong turn on the path back to her aunt and uncle. Desperation clawed at her as she hastened her pace, scanning the area for any sign of a safe haven.

As the wind howled around her, she rounded a bend, and the sight that met her eyes filled her with both relief and trepidation. Before her stood a grand manor house, imposing and elegant, a stark contrast to the wild, untamed landscape that surrounded it. The dark clouds overhead cast a shadow over the estate, lending it an air of mystery.

Gathering her courage, Elizabeth approached the house, her heart pounding in her chest. The first raindrops began to fall, and she rapped urgently on the heavy wooden door, her thoughts a whirlwind of uncertainty.

The door opened moments later, revealing the kindly face of an elderly housekeeper. "Please, do come in, Miss," she said, taking in Elizabeth's disheveled appearance with an understanding smile. "You must be seeking shelter from the storm. I am Mrs. Reynolds, the housekeeper of Pemberley."

Upon hearing the name 'Pemberley,' Elizabeth's eyes widened with a mixture of horror and embarrassment as she was all too aware of its connection to the enigmatic Mr. Darcy. Her mind raced back to their last encounter at Hunsford when she had vehemently rejected his arrogant proposal of marriage. Her cheeks flushed with the memory, and she felt a sudden, overwhelming sense of dread.

"Thank you, Mrs. Reynolds," she replied hesitantly, her voice barely concealing the turmoil of emotions that threatened to overwhelm her.

She stepped inside the warm and inviting home, desperately hoping that her presence would go unnoticed by its enigmatic master. "I am indeed grateful for your hospitality," she added, forcing a polite smile as she attempted to regain her composure in the face of this most unexpected and disconcerting turn of events.

As the heavy door closed behind her, Elizabeth found herself standing in the grand entrance hall of Pemberley. The housekeeper eyed Elizabeth with concern, noting her damp and disheveled state.

"Miss, you must be chilled to the bone," she exclaimed, her voice filled with genuine warmth.

"Allow me to show you to a guest room where you can change into dry clothes and warm yourself by the crackling fire."

"Thank you, Mrs. Reynolds," Elizabeth replied with gratitude as she hugged herself tightly, feeling the icy tendrils of cold creeping through her bones. "Your kindness is most appreciated. Could you also send a note to my aunt and uncle, the Gardiners? I would not want them to worry. We were visiting the Thornhills nearby when I got lost in this accursed storm."

"Of course, Miss Bennet, but it will have to wait until this tempest lessens," said Mrs. Reynolds, her kind eyes peering at Elizabeth with understanding.

As Elizabeth settled into the comforts of Pemberley, her mind was awash with thoughts of Mr. Darcy and the possibility of a chance encounter with him. Despite the grandeur and elegance of the estate, her heart fluttered with anxiety, making her feel like an intruder in the very place that had so graciously offered her shelter.

She recalled, however, the words of the innkeeper's servant at Lambton, who had mentioned in passing that the Darcy family was away for the summer. This knowledge provided some solace, but Elizabeth could not shake the nagging feeling that fate had a way of intertwining their paths in the most unexpected of circumstances.

As they ascended the sweeping staircase, Mrs. Reynolds informed Elizabeth that, by a twist of fate, Mr. Darcy had arrived at the estate just the day before and was currently present.

This revelation sent a jolt through Elizabeth's heart, her previous sense of security now shattered by the knowledge that Mr. Darcy was indeed within the walls of Pemberley. Her pulse quickened, and she couldn't help but feel a mixture of apprehension and intrigue at the thought of encountering him once again.

"Indeed, Miss Bennet," continued Mrs. Reynolds, seemingly oblivious to Elizabeth's sudden discomfort. "Mr. Darcy returned unexpectedly due to urgent matters that required his attention. It seems he decided to postpone his summer travels."

As they ascended the sweeping staircase, Elizabeth's mind whirled with the implications of this unexpected turn of events. The odds of their crossing paths at Pemberley were slim, yet here they were.

Was it mere coincidence or the machinations of fate? She couldn't deny that her curiosity was piqued, though her fear of an awkward reunion gnawed at the back of her mind.

Sensing Elizabeth's discomfort, Mrs. Reynolds kindly reassured her. "Do not worry, Miss Bennet. Mr. Darcy is a true gentleman and will undoubtedly understand your predicament. After all, it is not every day that a storm such as this descends upon our peaceful countryside."

Elizabeth attempted a smile, though it was tinged with trepidation. "Thank you, Mrs. Reynolds. Your words are most comforting," she replied, her voice betraying a hint of the anxiety that gripped her. As they made their way down the hallway, the scent of fresh roses wafted toward them, and Elizabeth couldn't help but feel a sense of awe at the opulence of her surroundings.

The housekeeper, Mrs. Reynolds, led Elizabeth down a lavishly decorated hallway lined with opulent tapestries and exquisite paintings. The walls were alive with vibrant colors, and the intricate details of each painting seemed to leap out at her. The grandeur of the estate was nothing short of breathtaking, a true testament to the wealth and status of its owner. Elizabeth couldn't help but stare in awe at her surroundings; it was a stark contrast to the simple abode of her own family.

At last, they arrived at a door leading to a luxurious guest room. As the door creaked open, an inviting warmth spread throughout the hallway. Inside, the fire had just been lit, casting a welcoming glow over the tastefully furnished space. The room was awash in soft light, and the flickering flames danced shadows across the walls. Elizabeth felt the chill of the air slowly dissipate as she stepped into the room.

"Here you are, Miss Bennet," said Mrs. Reynolds, gesturing towards the bed where a set of fresh clothes lay. "I have taken the liberty of laying out some dry clothes for you. If you require anything else, please do not hesitate to ask."

The chamber was elegantly furnished, with delicate floral patterns adorning the walls and a magnificent four-poster bed draped in luxurious silks. Elizabeth could feel the softness of the bedspread under her fingertips and the cool touch of the satin pillows against her cheek. The fire cast a warm glow over the room, offering solace from the frigid air that had seeped into Elizabeth's bones.

"Thank you, Mrs. Reynolds. You have been most kind," replied Elizabeth gratefully.

"I will have a hot bath sent up shortly, then come to the dining room for a warm meal," said Mrs. Reynolds before leaving the room.

Once alone, Elizabeth allowed herself to take in the unexpected turn her visit to Pemberley had taken. Her emotions were a tempest of anxiety, anticipation, and self-doubt. She paced around the room, her steps echoing softly on the hardwood floorboards, her thoughts consumed by the prospect of facing Mr. Darcy again. Would he be cold and aloof, his pride wounded by her rejection at Hunsford? Or had time and distance tempered his feelings, allowing for a more amicable reunion?

With a deep breath, Elizabeth steeled herself for the uncertainty that lay ahead. She knew that there was no avoiding Mr. Darcy during her stay at Pemberley, but perhaps this unexpected encounter would provide an opportunity for them to reconcile their past differences and forge a new understanding.

After luxuriating in a steaming bath and donning a serviceable but outdated gown, Elizabeth paused at the threshold and inhaled deeply, steadying her racing heart before stepping into the grand hallway. The opulent surroundings took her breath away, filled with tasteful elegance that perfectly reflected Pemberley's master - an artful blend of refined sophistication and understated charm. Its warmth and comfort seeped into her soul, easing her apprehension.

Paintings lining the walls and magnificent sculptures told stories of the Darcy family's long and storied history, stretching back for generations. Each piece whispered secrets from Mr. Darcy's past, piquing Elizabeth's curiosity and sparking her desire to learn more about the enigmatic gentleman.

As she descended the grand staircase, soft strains of music wafted through the air, soothing and enchanting. Intrigued, her heart pounding with each step, she followed the melody until it led her to an open door revealing an opulent drawing room. The fine paintings and gilded mirrors adorning the walls paled in comparison to the sight that met her eyes.

There, at the far end of the room, sat none other than Mr. Darcy, his nimble fingers expertly caressing the keys of a grand piano. The deep, rich notes reverberated through her very being, stirring a tempest of emotions that both horrified and captivated her. As the music swelled, the distance between them seemed to shrink, casting a powerful spell that drew Elizabeth closer to him.

Mesmerized by the graceful movements of his skilled fingers dancing across the ivory keys, Elizabeth was enraptured. The room shrank around them as the music wove a sensual cocoon, enveloping them in its magic. Their palpable tension left her pulse racing with a mixture of trepidation and desire.

CHAPTER 2

*E*lizabeth stood frozen, her mind racing with a mixture of shock and embarrassment, as Mr. Darcy's fingers glided gracefully across the ivory keys. The elegant melodies that filled the room were drowned out by the pounding of her heart in her ears. She knew she should turn and leave, make her escape before he noticed her intrusion, but an inexplicable force held her rooted to the spot. Her eyes were unable to tear themselves away from the captivating figure before her.

Unaware of Elizabeth's presence, Mr. Darcy continued playing, his broad shoulders and long, elegant fingers confidently tickling the ivory keys. The music echoed the melancholy that seemed to envelop him. He appeared before her as a complex and sensitive soul, stirring feelings she had never anticipated.

As the final notes of the haunting melody drifted through the air, Mr. Darcy's fingers stilled, and he let out a deep, weary sigh. It was then that he finally sensed her presence, his eyes lifting to meet hers.

The sudden shock and recognition that flashed across his features mirrored her own, and for a brief moment, time seemed to stand still. Awareness crackled between them, potent and intoxicating as fine wine.

Elizabeth felt the weight of his gaze move over her like a caress, leaving her powerless under the intensity of his stare. She drew in a sharp breath, her lips parting in anticipation of she knew not what.

"Miss Bennet," he whispered, his voice barely audible over the pounding of her heart. "I—I did not expect to see you here."

Elizabeth swallowed nervously, her cheeks flushing with embarrassment and desire. "Mr. Darcy," she managed to stammer, her words trembling with the weight of the emotions that threatened to consume her. "I... I did not intend to intrude, Mr. Darcy. I was caught in the storm and sought shelter here."

The scent of pine and spice enveloped her as he rose from the piano bench and crossed the room to stand before her. "There is no need for apologies. I am simply... surprised to see you."

As their eyes locked, Elizabeth felt the world around her fade away, leaving only the two of them suspended in a moment of vulnerability and unexpected connection. The air between them seemed to crackle with unspoken emotion, the echoes of their shared past mingling with the uncertainty of the present. Elizabeth knew that she should leave, yet found herself unable to move, caught in the web of emotions that bound them together.

Mr. Darcy shifted uncomfortably, the weight of their prolonged silence pressing down upon them. It seemed as though he was searching for the right words, his eyes briefly flickering to the side before returning to hers. The heat in his gaze left her trembling, awakening a hunger. "I trust your family is well, Miss Bennet?" he inquired, his tone husky yet tentative, testing the waters of their newfound connection.

"Yes, Mr. Darcy," she whispered, her voice trembling. "They are quite well, thank you for asking." Elizabeth's cheeks flushed with embarrassment and desire, and she struggled to maintain her composure.

"And what brings you to Derbyshire, if I may ask?" he persisted, his voice gentle yet raw with longing, as if afraid of shattering the fragile bond between them.

"I am accompanying my aunt and uncle, the Gardiners, on a countryside excursion," Elizabeth explained, her voice steadier now. "They have friends in the area, so we decided to take advantage of the beautiful scenery."

As they spoke, Elizabeth found herself studying Mr. Darcy with newfound interest. The man before her was a far cry from the arrogant, aloof gentleman she had once known. Instead, she saw a man who was kind, thoughtful, and perhaps even a little shy in his attempts to engage her in conversation. Yet beneath the gentlemanly facade, she sensed a barely restrained passion that set her blood ablaze.

The storm outside intensified, the sound of raindrops pummeling against the windows adding an air of intimacy to their conversation. The room felt charged with energy, leaving Elizabeth trembling in its wake. The tempest mirrored the turbulence of their emotions, the ferocity of the winds echoing the unspoken desire that stirred within them.

"Miss Bennet, might I inquire about the whereabouts of your aunt and uncle?" Mr. Darcy asked, furrowing his brow in concern as he recalled her earlier explanation of being alone in Derbyshire.

"They remain at our friends' house," Elizabeth replied, her cheeks flushing slightly at the realization of how her solitary exploration might be viewed. "I decided to take a walk and, quite unexpectedly, found myself here."

Mr. Darcy's eyes widened, admiration mingling with desire at her daring spirit. "I must admit, I am impressed by your courage, Miss Bennet. Walking alone in such weather is no small feat. However, I am concerned for your well-being. Might I suggest we retire to the dining room so you can partake in some refreshment?"

Elizabeth, touched by his concern, agreed, and they made their way to the dining room. As they entered, the soft glow of candlelight illuminated the elegantly laid table, creating a warm and intimate atmosphere. Mr. Darcy pulled out a chair for her, his fingers grazing her bare skin and igniting sparks that raced through her veins. Elizabeth sat down, acutely aware of his heated gaze.

He hesitated before taking a seat at the opposite end of the table, his eyes never leaving hers. The air between them crackled with tension, the silence punctuated only by the sound of the storm raging outside.

As Elizabeth ate, she stole glances at Mr. Darcy, her heart racing at the intensity of his gaze. The memory of their earlier conversation played through her mind, the recollection of his kind words and gentle demeanor softening her perception of the man she had once vehemently disliked. And the memory of his sensual tones and smoldering looks awakened a hunger she had never known.

Mr. Darcy cast a concerned glance towards the window, where the storm continued to rage on relentlessly. "Miss Bennet, I fear the tempest shows no inclination to abate. It would be most imprudent for you to venture forth under such inclement circumstances. Please allow me to insist that you remain here until the storm passes."

Anticipation bubbled within Elizabeth's chest as she contemplated the thought of spending the night at

Pemberley, alone with the enigmatic Mr. Darcy. A shiver ran down her spine, and her heart skipped a beat as he rose from his chair, a hint of eagerness lighting up his countenance.

"Miss Bennet, as you shall be our guest for a while, might I propose a tour of Pemberley? I would be honored to acquaint you with some of the estate's most cherished features," he said, holding out an arm in invitation.

As they strolled through the grand halls and exquisite chambers of Pemberley, Mr. Darcy regaled Elizabeth with tales of his childhood and the storied history of the estate. The opulent furnishings and ornate decorations, bathed in the soft glow of candlelight, only served to heighten the romantic atmosphere surrounding them.

With each room they entered, Mr. Darcy's voice grew softer, his gaze lingering on Elizabeth's face a little longer than before. The unspoken message behind his words left her trembling with desire, her heart racing in her chest.

Mr. Darcy's tender touches and intense gazes grew bolder and more intimate as they spent more time together. Their fingertips brushed against one another as they admired the fine details of the art on the walls, or he placed a gentle hand on the small of her back to guide her through the many rooms of Pemberley. Each subtle gesture sent a thrill through Elizabeth, making her pulse race and her cheeks flush with color.

In the Pemberley library, Mr. Darcy reached up to take down a book, his arm brushing ever so softly against Elizabeth's shoulder. Her skin tingled where he touched her, and she found it difficult to focus on anything other than the tantalizing closeness of his body. "I must confess," Mr. Darcy began hesitantly, as they entered a room filled with exquisite paintings and sculptures, "that I have always dreamed of using my wealth and influence to make a meaningful difference in the world, to provide opportunities for those less fortunate."

Elizabeth, surprised by his admission, replied with genuine curiosity, "That is a noble aspiration, Mr. Darcy. And what sort of opportunities do you envision?"

As he paused, deep in thought, his hand brushed against hers, sending a jolt of sensation through her entire being. "I would like to support education and the arts, as well as create programs that empower individuals to improve their own lives and communities."

"How admirable," Elizabeth said, her voice slightly breathless. "I have always believed that education is the key to unlocking one's potential."

Their conversation flowed on, deepening the connection between them as they shared their most intimate thoughts. The simmering tension between them intensified with each passing moment as they sat close together.

"And what of you, Miss Bennet?" Mr. Darcy inquired softly, his voice laced with tenderness. "What secret dreams do you hold close to your heart?"

Elizabeth's cheeks reddened, but she spoke confi-dently, "I long to travel and explore the world beyond Hertfordshire. I would like to experience different cultures and perhaps write about my adventures."

As Mr. Darcy gazed at her lips, he whispered, "You would make an extraordinary travel writer, Eliza-beth. Your sharp wit and exceptional observations will capture the essence of every place you visit."

The air around them crackled with tension as their shared hopes and desires forged a bond that neither saw coming.

As they walked through the opulent drawing room, their hands brushed against each other accidentally, igniting a delicious shiver down both their spines. Every time their eyes met, they held each other's gaze for just one moment longer than was appropriate, an unspoken understanding passing between them as they surrendered to their growing attraction.

Outside, the storm raged on, contrasting the intimate dance of passion unfolding within the walls of Pemberley. The flickering candlelight and crackling fire created a warm and inviting atmosphere as Elizabeth, and Mr. Darcy continued exploring their feelings for each other. The stolen touches and lingering glances quickened their hearts, leaving them breathless and wanting.

"In truth," Mr. Darcy admitted as they stood before the grand fireplace, "I have felt isolated by my position and responsibilities. To share my thoughts and dreams with someone who understands me is an immeasurable gift."

Touched by his sincerity, Elizabeth placed her hand gently on his arm, feeling the heat radiating from him. "I understand, Mr. Darcy, and I am grateful for the connection we share."

In the quiet of the music room, Mr. Darcy stood behind Elizabeth as she played the pianoforte, his fingers brushing lightly against hers on the keys. The shared melodies seemed to mirror their unspoken desire, the notes hanging in the air like a whispered confession.

Despite the propriety demanded of them, the smoldering glances and delicate touches only served to fuel the flames of passion burning within them. As they wandered through the halls of Pemberley together, they found themselves drawn closer and closer, the boundaries between them becoming increasingly blurred. The subtle dance of intimacy and desire that played out between them deepened their connection, leaving them both yearning for more.

CHAPTER 3

The day drew to a close, and Elizabeth found herself alone in the dimly lit library with Mr. Darcy. The flickering candles cast a warm glow upon the rows of leather-bound volumes while the air was heavy with the weight of their unspoken feelings. Outside, the storm raged on, the wind howling and the rain lashing against the windows with ferocity.

As they stood mere inches apart, their breaths mingling in the charged air between them, Elizabeth felt her heart racing, her pulse pounding in her ears like the relentless drumbeat of the storm. She could feel the warmth radiating from Mr. Darcy's body, an aching reminder of the barriers that still separated them.

"I must confess, Miss Bennet," Mr. Darcy whispered, his voice barely audible over the cacophony of the storm, "I have been unable to banish you from my thoughts since our last encounter. Your presence here at Pemberley has only served to intensify my feelings."

Elizabeth's breath caught in her throat, her eyes widening in surprise and something akin to fear. She had never dared to imagine that Mr. Darcy might share her own feelings, and the revelation left her feeling dizzy with a heady mix of elation and uncertainty.

"Mr. Darcy," she replied hesitantly, her voice quivering with emotion, "I must admit that I, too, have found myself unable to forget our previous encounters. Your kindness and understanding have shown me a side of you that I had not anticipated, and I find myself drawn to you in a way I cannot fully explain."

The intensity of his gaze never wavered, his eyes dark and full of longing as he reached out a trembling hand to gently cup her cheek. His touch sent shivers down her spine, igniting a fire within her that threatened to consume her entirely.

The intensity of Mr. Darcy's gaze burned into Elizabeth, dark and full of promise. He stood close enough for her to feel the warmth of his breath on her cheek yet still maintained an appropriate distance.

"Elizabeth," he murmured, his voice heavy with desire and barely audible above the howling winds outside, "if you will allow me, I would like nothing more than to explore these feelings that have taken hold of us both."

His words, full of longing and vulnerability, sent shivers down her spine. As the storm raged around them, Elizabeth found herself unable to resist the magnetic pull of his smoldering gaze and the promise of forbidden pleasure. She hesitated, her breath catching in her throat, before she finally whispered, "Yes, Mr. Darcy."

Elizabeth trembled in anticipation as Mr. Darcy closed the distance between them, his eyes never leaving hers. Every passing second seemed to linger interminably, her breath held in anticipation until, at last, their lips met in a tender, passionate kiss that seemed to ignite every nerve in her body.

As their mouths moved together, Mr. Darcy's hand gently cupped her cheek while the other rested at the small of her back, drawing her closer until she was pressed tightly against him. Whatever barriers had existed between them before had been reduced to mere wisps of memory as they clung to one another in an embrace of pure desire and longing.

They broke apart, gasping for air. Elizabeth's heart pounded in her chest as she gazed into Mr. Darcy's eyes. Time seemed to stand still as they clung to each other, seeking comfort from the storm outside.

"Elizabeth," Mr. Darcy murmured huskily, his thumb caressing her cheek ever so softly as he leaned forward once again to brush his lips against hers in a feather-light kiss.

The rest of the world melted away around them; all that remained was this perfect moment filled with emotion and promise. Elizabeth felt herself blossom under his touch--all fear and hesitation replaced by an indescribable joy that seemed to fill her entire being with its warmth and light.

The world around them seemed to fade into shadow and candlelight, leaving only the two of them in this intimate moment.

As they surrendered to the depths of their passion, they treaded cautiously into uncharted realms of ecstasy, their stolen kisses and forbidden touches an intoxicating dance that mirrored the storm outside. The boundaries of propriety blurred, and they were swept away in a maelstrom of longing and desire, the intensity of their feelings outshining even the tempest that raged beyond Pemberley's walls.

The library was their sanctuary, filled with the scent of old leather and musty pages. The flickering candlelight cast long shadows across the room, bathing them in an amber glow. Each caress spurred them on to greater heights of pleasure as they sought to slake the hunger that only grew more ravenous with each fevered kiss.

Elizabeth gasped into his mouth as his hands roamed freely over her body, slipping beneath layers of silk and lace to tease her sensitive skin. She clung to him, her fingers twisting in the fabric of his coat as a delicious ache built within her, winding tighter until she thought she might shatter from sheer need.

He whispered words of love and desire as he explored her body, igniting a fierce hunger within her that threatened to consume her whole. She surrendered to his touch, arching against him as he teased her with his caresses.

His touch inflamed her, eliciting a soft moan as he explored every inch of her curves with a passionate intensity that left her trembling and panting in anticipation. She eagerly returned his caresses, eagerly tasting and exploring every part of him with unrestrained desire.

The heat between them threatened to consume them both--each movement intensifying the fire that burned within until Elizabeth felt herself surrendering to its power. Mr. Darcy's mouth moved hungrily over hers as he tracked blazing kisses down the length of her neck and across her collarbone, his hands never ceasing their exploration.

"So responsive," he purred against her lips. "I wonder how you shall fare when I strip you bare and lavish you with the attention you so richly deserve."

"Mr. Darcy," she moaned, trembling at the images his words evoked. She could scarce draw breath, so consumed was she by longing for his possession of her in all ways. "I ache for your touch... your kiss..."

In that moment, nothing else mattered. The storm outside could rage on, tearing at the walls of

Pemberley. But here, in this intimate embrace, Elizabeth and Mr. Darcy were worlds away from everything else, lost in a haze of desire and love.

Their fingers traced teasing paths over heated skin, igniting sparks that raced through their veins and fueling the flames of passion. With each touch, Mr. Darcy felt himself being pulled deeper into the depths of sensual pleasure, unable to resist Elizabeth's seductive charms any longer. His mouth sought out her delectable curves as he indulged in her sweetness, every kiss setting his soul ablaze with longing for more.

Elizabeth trembled beneath his touch, drowning in the depths of desire that shone in his darkened gaze. She marveled at how this man, once thought cold and unfeeling, had awakened her to pleasure beyond imagining. Now, as his skillful caresses brought her ever closer to ecstasy, she saw the truth of his longing laid bare before her. This was no aloof gentleman but a man consumed by love and hungering for the woman who held his heart.

She gasped as his hand slid between her thighs once more, his fingers stroking and teasing until she thought she might shatter. "So beautiful like this," he purred, brushing his lips against her neck as she writhed beneath him. "When you come undone for me, I can scarce restrain myself..." His words trailed off into a low growl, and Elizabeth felt the ridge of his arousal pressed insistently against her.

"Then do not," she breathed, looping her arms around his neck and pulling his mouth back to hers. She kissed him with abandon, seeking to convey her longing through touch alone.

He groaned into her mouth, his restraint slipping further with each stolen caress. When at last she cried out her release, shattering around his clever fingers, he could hold back no longer.

With trembling hands, he undressed her slowly, revealing smooth ivory skin and delicate curves that begged to be touched and explored. Her soft moans only drove him on as he worked his way down her body, exposing hidden treasures that no other had seen before. He ravaged her with gentle kisses and passionate caresses, coaxing cries of pleasure from deep within her throat until she melted against him in complete surrender.

Elizabeth reveled in the sensory overload of his touch. She felt the roughness of his hands moving across her silken skin, leaving behind trails of heat wherever they roamed. The scent of sandalwood mingled with the musky aroma of desire, creating a heady perfume that filled the air around them. His lips were everywhere at once, trailing along the curve of her neck, nipping at her earlobes, and claiming her mouth with fierce possession.

As Mr. Darcy's hands roamed possessively over Elizabeth's body, her senses were on fire with the feverish desire that had been building between them for so long. She writhed beneath him in a blissful abandon, her breath quickening with each touch of his lips as they teased and tantalized sensitive places on her body. Waves of pleasure coursed through her veins as every stroke and caress ignited an insatiable hunger for more.

Elizabeth's body trembled with both passion and uncertainty, but she trusted the love that would guide them.

"Do not fear, my darling," he whispered tenderly, soothing her with a soft kiss to her brow. "I shall bring you only pleasure."

With infinite care, he eased her open, breaching her innocence and claiming her irrevocably as his own. There was pain, brief and fleeting, then ecstasy such as she had never known. He moved slowly, tenderly stroking her until she opened to him like a flower in the sun. She felt herself blossom under his touch, a new and powerful need overtaking her body and soul as sensations of pleasure overwhelmed her.

Mr. Darcy's words of love were both tender and passionate as he explored every inch of Elizabeth's body with hands that knew no bounds. He left no stone unturned, caressing and teasing until she quivered beneath him in pleasure. His lips blazed a trail up her neck to her ear, where he whispered sweet nothings that only stoked the fire burning inside her. When his tongue flicked against the sensitive spot behind her earlobe, she gasped in delight at the sizzling sensation that shot through her veins.

He found her most sensitive places and stroked them with perfect precision, heightening her pleasure to dizzying heights she had never before experienced. With each passing moment, their passion escalated until Elizabeth was lost in an exquisite haze of blissful desire.

His deep desire for her was palpable, and it drove him on as their bodies joined in perfect harmony. Elizabeth felt herself melding into him as wave after wave of pleasure coursed through them both -

sending them soaring beyond the heights they had ever dreamed of reaching together.

They moved together, hearts beating in unison and souls entwined as if they were one being. Elizabeth cried out in joy as she felt Mr. Darcy's immense pleasure joining hers, creating an exquisite bliss that seemed to last forever before finally ebbing away into a contented peace.

The storm still raged beyond their sanctuary, but within its hallowed walls, their future stretched out endlessly, lit by the glow of love and warmed by passion's flame.

Their fingers traced gentle patterns on each other's skin, sending shivers down their spines and igniting a fire that burned brightly within their hearts.

Elizabeth marveled at the depth of her feelings for Mr. Darcy, a man she had once thought cold and unfeeling. Now, she saw the warmth and tenderness that lay beneath his aloof exterior, the passion that had been hidden from her for so long.

She trembled, drowning in the depths of desire that shone in his darkened gaze, and marveled at how this man, once thought cold and unfeeling, had awakened her to pleasure beyond imagining. Elizabeth felt as though she was seeing him for the first time, her heart swelling with love and gratitude for the man who had shown her the true meaning of love and devotion.

"Mr. Darcy," Elizabeth whispered, her voice filled with wonder and affection.

"Call me Fitzwilliam," he whispered.

"Fitzwilliam, I never imagined that my heart could feel so full, so complete. This love that has blossomed between us is unlike anything I have ever known."

He smiled tenderly, brushing a stray curl from her forehead and placing a gentle kiss upon her brow. "My dearest Elizabeth, you have awakened in me a love that I had never dared to dream possible. I cannot imagine my life without you, and I pray that you will allow me the honor of sharing in this incredible journey with you for as long as we both shall live."

Their lips met then with whispered oaths and tender sighs, seeking and finding in sweet abandon that sacred place where two hearts become one. The fire of their passion burned brightly, warming the lovers nestled close against the gathering dark.

CHAPTER 4

The storm raged on outside the sturdy walls of Pemberley, but within the library, a fire crackled and popped in the hearth, casting flickering shadows across the room. Mr. Darcy's warm breath tickled Elizabeth's ear as he whispered her name, his fingers trailing feather-light touches down her arm. She shivered with delight, her heart racing as he tilted her chin up to gaze into her eyes.

"Elizabeth," he murmured, his voice husky with desire. "If only I could keep you here in my arms forever, I would count myself the happiest of men."

Her pulse quickened at his words, her fingers twisting gently in his hair as she breathed out a sigh of contentment. Mr. Darcy groaned deep in his chest, the sound igniting fresh desire that she knew would keep them tangled in passion's embrace until dawn.

The tempest raged outside the sturdy walls of Pemberley, but within, a fire of passion burned hotter than any storm. The rooms of the grand estate became their playground as they explored each other with hands and lips, no space left unconquered in their quest to know every secret hollow and plane of the other's body. Breathless, they tore at each other's clothes, so lost to their desire that they scarcely noticed the echo of approaching footsteps outside the room.

Only the creak of the opening door spared them from being discovered in a passionate embrace, and they sprang apart just as the housekeeper entered.

Elizabeth's cheeks flamed as she fumbled to straighten her disheveled skirts and hair, acutely aware of how they must have appeared. She dared not meet Mr. Darcy's gaze, afraid of betraying just how much his kiss had affected her.

The housekeeper paused, her eyes flickering between them for a probing moment before she continued about her business. Elizabeth breathed a quiet sigh of relief while Mr. Darcy raked a hand through his mussed hair, color rising in his own cheeks.

Once the housekeeper had gone, Mr. Darcy turned burning eyes to Elizabeth, the intensity of his gaze setting her blood aflame once more. "That was too close," he growled, striding forward to pull her fiercely into his arms. "I will not risk almost losing you again. Being with you has made me lose all reason and restraint. To taste your lips, to hold you in my arms, is all I have dreamt of since we met."

Elizabeth sighed breathlessly as his mouth claimed hers once more, their kiss as passionate as before. "Then we must retire to somewhere more private," she managed between kisses.

A low groan rumbled in his throat as he swept her up into his arms. "I could not agree more."

He carried her effortlessly as he strode from the room with purposeful strides. Elizabeth's heart raced as she tucked her face into the crook of his neck, breathing in his familiar scent of crisp linen and sandalwood, the feel of his muscles rippling beneath his shirt sending shivers down her spine.

The marble stairs of Pemberley stretched endlessly before them, every step fueling her anticipation as they drew closer to his bedchamber. By the time they reached the top of the stairs, her lips were tingling from the fervent kisses he had trailed down the column of her throat, and she was trembling with need.

The ornate oak door to his bedchamber loomed before them, and with a swift movement, Mr. Darcy opened it and strode inside, kicking the door shut behind them. Elizabeth's eyes fixed on the massive four-poster bed draped in emerald silk, her breath quickening at the thought of what was to come.

He smiled down at her with a devastating mixture of tenderness and desire. "And now, my love," he purred, "we are alone."

Lowering his lips to hers, their kiss deepened into raw passion as he gently bore her down onto the bed. Elizabeth gasped, clinging to him tightly, as a maelstrom of sensation overwhelmed her. His hands and mouth seemed to be everywhere at once, setting her blood aflame as they traced the edge of her chemise and skimmed down the column of her throat.

As their lips parted, Mr. Darcy gazed down at her with dark, hooded eyes. "Every touch, every kiss, has been but a prelude to this, my darling. Tonight I will worship you as you deserve."

She trembled beneath the intensity of his gaze, her body thrumming with desire she had never known. "Yes," she breathed. "Tonight, I am yours."

Mr. Darcy's lips curved into a devastating smile as he continued to gaze down at her with smoldering eyes. "As I am yours, Elizabeth..."

The promise in his words echoing the same vow in his searing kiss ignited her passion until she was consumed by its flames. His hands roamed her body with reverent touches, stripping away her garments one precious layer at a time. Elizabeth trembled beneath his loving caresses, her soft cries of pleasure absorbed by his seeking mouth.

When at last she lay bare before him, he drew back to admire her with a low growl of longing. "Exquisite," he breathed.

She flushed at the raw desire in his gaze, turning her head to shy away even as her body ached for his touch.

Gently, he tilted her chin up and feathered kisses along the graceful arch of her neck. "Do not hide yourself from me, my love," he whispered. "You are beautiful beyond words."

His tender reassurance emboldened her, and she pulled him close, relishing in the solid strength of his embrace. Their kisses deepened into a slow, seductive rhythm that stoked the fires of passion until all that remained was a primal, aching need. Carefully, his hands traversed her flushed skin. She sighed with pleasure as his weight pressed deliciously against her own.

"Elizabeth..." Her name was a reverent sigh upon his lips as their bodies joined, shattering the last of her doubts.

She wrapped herself around him, drawing him impossibly close as they moved together. Never had she known such bliss, and if this was to be the only night she would share with him, she would make it a memory to last forever.

Elizabeth cried out in ecstasy as Fitzwilliam quickened his pace, her fingers twisting into the luxurious bedding. He claimed her mouth in a searing kiss, muffling her cries as he drove her higher to the pinnacle of pleasure and beyond.

When at last they lay spent in each other's arms, their harsh breathing slowly calming, Elizabeth nestled against his chest, overcome with love and tenderness for the man who had so unexpectedly won her heart. She traced idle patterns across his skin, delighting in the texture of him, warm and flushed in the aftermath of their passion.

"I love you," she whispered, finally speaking aloud the emotion that had taken hold of her soul. "With all my heart, I love you, Fitzwilliam."

He held her tightly, pressing his lips tenderly against her hair. "As I love you, Elizabeth," he murmured. "This is not mere lust or fleeting desire. You have claimed my heart today and forever."

Joy flooded through her, bright and golden like the sun breaking through the clouds. She lifted her gaze to meet his, finding the truth of his feelings in the depths of his eyes. "Forever is a promise I would ask no man to make," she breathed. "Yet from you, Fitzwilliam, I would accept nothing less."

A gentle smile curved his lips as he reached out to caress her cheek. "Then you have my heart, my love, and my eternal devotion, now and always." His eyes shone with affection as he gazed down at her, brimming with love and tender promise. "There is no part of my life, no segment of my soul, that does not belong to you. You are my wife, my heart, my home...my everything."

"As you are mine," she whispered. Joy and tears mingled as she drew him down for another searing kiss, knowing that she had discovered her fate – and her heart's true haven.

Their passion was temporarily quenched but always smoldering for more. As rain pelted against the windows, Elizabeth traced idle patterns across the solid muscles of his chest, her body snuggled contentedly against his side.

"It appears I will need to summon more storms if this is the outcome," Mr. Darcy said, his lips curling into a devastating smile as he looked down at her with eyes darkened by passion.

Elizabeth chuckled, tilting her head up to claim his mouth again. "I doubt Pemberley could survive many more days like this," she teased. "The estate may not withstand us, Mr. Darcy."

"Then we shall have to explore other places," he countered, pulling her on top to straddle her hips. "For there are many rooms and many places left to be christened."

Elizabeth gazed at the man she adored, her heart overflowing with joy. However wild the storm outside, the tempest within was far more powerful, and she knew that she would gladly ride it to whatever end.

THE FIRST RAYS of dawn streamed through the windows, casting a soft glow upon the intertwined forms slumbering together. Elizabeth stirred, waking up to a world transformed by the love she and Fitzwilliam had shared the night before. She stretched lazily, feeling a pleasant ache in her body from their ardent exploration, and smiled at the man beside her. Fitzwilliam's eyes opened, and he smiled back, pulling her closer.

"Greetings, my love," he whispered, pressing his lips gently against her forehead. Elizabeth basked in the warmth of his embrace for a few more moments before they were interrupted by the harsh reality of the day.

As they readied themselves to depart their chamber, a sudden fear crept into Elizabeth's mind. "Fitzwilliam," she murmured hesitantly, "do you think the servants will ever discuss our... intimacy?"

He looked at her with compassion, his eyes brimming with affection. "My dear Elizabeth, the staff at Pemberley are devoted and discreet. They have served my family for generations and comprehend that the private lives of their employers are off-limits for gossip."

Elizabeth nodded, comforted by his words, but a trace of unease lingered within her. It was one thing to know that their love was a matter of utmost secrecy; it was another to face the people who, though quiet, would be privy to the most intimate aspects of their existence.

Reluctantly, they rose from their bed and dressed, the mundane tasks of the morning serving as a poignant reminder of the world beyond their bedroom door. As they descended the grand staircase together, hand in hand, Elizabeth couldn't help but marvel at the transformation in Mr. Darcy's demeanor. The haughty, aloof man she had once known was gone, replaced by a tender, adoring partner who reveled in every word and touch.

They enjoyed breakfast together in the morning room, exchanging warm smiles and gentle caresses, their conversation playful and teasing despite the raging storm outside.

Suddenly, the sound of the tempest interrupted their intimate repartee. They turned to each other in surprise as they realized that the front door had opened amidst the squall, and the faint murmur of a voice reached their ears.

Curious and concerned, they rose from their seats and made their way to the entrance hall, where they were astonished to find Mr. Darcy's cousin, Colonel Fitzwilliam. The charming and dashing officer, soaked to the bone, grinned warmly as he greeted them.

"Forgive me, dear cousin," he said, shaking water from his hat. "I hadn't anticipated arriving in the midst of such a storm."

Mr. Darcy, taken aback by his cousin's unanticipated arrival, managed a smile. "Your presence is always welcome, Richard. But how did you manage to brave this tempest?"

"The roads were treacherous, but my horse is a sturdy creature," Colonel Fitzwilliam replied with a grin. "I'm relieved to have arrived safely."

As the butler fetched dry clothes and a towel for Colonel Fitzwilliam, both Elizabeth and Mr. Darcy felt a wave of nervousness wash over them. She had not expected anyone to find out about her liaison with Mr. Darcy.

Upon seeing Elizabeth, Colonel Fitzwilliam's eyes lit up with recognition. "Miss Bennet, what a pleasant surprise to see you again after our encounter at Rosings Park last year. I trust you have been well?"

Elizabeth offered a polite curtsy, endeavoring to remain composed despite her apprehension. "Indeed, Colonel Fitzwilliam, it is a pleasure to see you again. I have been well, thank you."

Realizing the need for clarification, Mr. Darcy interjected, "Richard, I must tell you that Miss Elizabeth Bennet and I have recently made a commitment to each other. She is not a mere guest at Pemberley but rather someone I hold dear and cherish."

Colonel Fitzwilliam raised an eyebrow but remained silent, his expression unreadable. He nodded as he took the towel from the butler, allowing his cousin's words to sink in.

As Colonel Fitzwilliam absorbed Mr. Darcy's words, Elizabeth felt a deep sense of unease. She was acutely aware that her behavior during her stay at Pemberley had not adhered to the strict rules of propriety that governed their society. The realization that Colonel Fitzwilliam, a man she respected and admired, now knew of her indiscretion weighed heavily on her conscience. She worried that his judgment of her character would be irrevocably tarnished.

Her cheeks flushed with embarrassment, and she nervously twisted her fingers in the fabric of her dress. She desperately wished she could take back the past few days and act with more decorum. Yet, she knew it was impossible, and the knowledge that she had potentially lost Colonel Fitzwilliam's esteem pained her deeply.

The tension in the entrance hall seemed to magnify Elizabeth's discomfort, and she could not help but steal furtive glances at Colonel Fitzwilliam, searching his expression for any hint of disapproval. Her heart thudded painfully in her chest as she awaited his reaction to Mr. Darcy's revelation, praying that their friendship could somehow remain unscathed.

CHAPTER 5

Colonel Fitzwilliam, after a moment's contemplation, let out a deep sigh. "Fitzwilliam," he began, his tone serious, "I understand that you may have developed strong feelings for Miss Bennet. However, you must be aware that having her as a mistress out in the open at Pemberley could have severe consequences for both your reputations."

Mr. Darcy bristled at his cousin's words, but before he could respond, Elizabeth stepped forward. "Colonel Fitzwilliam," she said with as much grace as she could muster, "I assure you that our feelings for one another are genuine, and we have no intention of causing any disgrace to either of our families."

Despite his surprise, Colonel Fitzwilliam responded with restraint. "Miss Bennet," he began, his gaze filled with astonishment, "when we last met at Rosings Park, I was most impressed by your wit, intelligence, and sense of propriety. I must admit, I am taken aback by the current situation."

His eyes flickered between Elizabeth and Mr. Darcy as if trying to reconcile the woman he had previously admired with the one who now stood before him. "You must understand appearances matter a great deal in our world, and as a gentleman, Fitzwilliam has certain responsibilities to uphold. I am truly surprised to find you both in this position."

Elizabeth's cheeks flushed with embarrassment, but her pride quickly gave way to indignation at Colonel Fitzwilliam's words. She lifted her chin and met his gaze, her voice firm as she spoke. "Colonel, I understand that you are concerned for both of our sakes, but I must remind you that we are not children to be scolded. We are aware of the potential consequences of our actions and have made our choices based on our feelings for one another."

Mr. Darcy, though also taken aback by his cousin's judgment, stepped forward in support of Elizabeth.

"Richard, while I value your counsel, I must ask you to trust that I have given this matter the consideration it deserves. Elizabeth and I have found happiness in each other, and I am prepared to stand by her, regardless of the opinions of others."

Colonel Fitzwilliam's gaze shifted between the pair, recognizing their determination.

The three of them stood in silence, the tension thickening as the storm outside raged on. Elizabeth's heart ached with the injustice of it all. The rain outside pummeled against the windows with the sound of a thousand tiny drums as she longed for a world where they could simply be together, free from the constraints of society's expectations.

Mr. Darcy, sensing Elizabeth's anguish, took her hand and squeezed it gently. "Richard," he said firmly, "I understand your concerns, but I cannot ignore what I feel for Elizabeth. I am willing to face the consequences of our actions, for she means more to me than any social convention ever could."

Colonel Fitzwilliam looked between his cousin and Elizabeth, the memory of their previous meeting at Rosings Park fresh in his mind. He had thought highly of Elizabeth then and was genuinely surprised by the turn of events. With a sigh, he nodded. "Very well," he said at last, "I cannot change your mind, but I implore you both to be cautious. Society can be cruel, and I would hate to see either of you suffer needlessly, especially considering my previous regard for you, Miss Bennet."

Elizabeth offered a small, grateful smile in response to Colonel Fitzwilliam's words, her heart still heavy with the weight of their predicament.

As Colonel Fitzwilliam excused himself to change into dry clothes, Mr. Darcy and Elizabeth exchanged concerned glances before returning to the breakfast table. They ate in silence, their thoughts consumed by the confrontation that had just taken place. Elizabeth's heart felt heavy, knowing that their love was being scrutinized by someone who had known her in a different context.

When Colonel Fitzwilliam returned, he found Mr. Darcy alone in the drawing room, deep in thought. Elizabeth had retreated to her room, leaving the two men to discuss their concerns privately.

"Tell me, Fitzwilliam," Colonel Fitzwilliam began, his tone gentle but firm, "what do you truly intend for

Miss Bennet? You must know that even the appearance of impropriety could bring scandal and ruin upon you both."

Mr. Darcy looked up, his eyes filled with determination. "I assure you, Richard, my intentions towards Elizabeth are honorable. I love her deeply, and I would do anything to protect her from harm."

Colonel Fitzwilliam regarded his cousin thoughtfully. "I understand that you may be blinded by your feelings for her, but you must consider the consequences of your actions, even if they were unintended."

Mr. Darcy bristled at his cousin's words. "I am well aware of the consequences, Richard, but I believe our love is worth the risk. We did not seek out this situation, but now that we have found each other again, I will not allow society's prejudices to dictate my happiness."

Colonel Fitzwilliam sighed, running a hand through his damp hair, which dripped onto the wooden floorboards. "Fitzwilliam, I care for you both, and it is because of that care that I must urge you to be cautious. Elizabeth is a remarkable woman, and I remember her fondly from our time at Rosings Park. However, you must consider how your actions could be compared to what Wickham has done to young women wherever he went. If you truly love Miss Bennet, you must find a way to honor her without tarnishing her reputation or your own."

Mr. Darcy stood, his eyes flashing with resolve. "Richard, I resent the comparison to Wickham. My love for Elizabeth is genuine, and I would never do anything to cause her harm. I appreciate your concern, but I am confident in the strength of our love. We will face whatever challenges may come together and with dignity," he said, his voice filled with conviction.

Colonel Fitzwilliam's face reddened, and he clenched his fists in frustration. "I am not questioning your love, Fitzwilliam, but you must understand that our society does not look kindly upon such arrangements. Your actions affect not only you but also those you claim to care for. Is it genuinely worth the potential ruin?"

"I refuse to let my love for Elizabeth be dictated by society's hypocritical standards," Mr. Darcy retorted. His jaw tightened, and he stared at his cousin with unwavering resolve. "I know the risks involved, but I am prepared to face them for her sake and mine."

Colonel Fitzwilliam shook his head, a mix of concern and exasperation etched in his expression. "You are a stubborn man, Fitzwilliam, but I fear your obstinacy may lead to your downfall in this matter. You cannot defy the world and expect to emerge unscathed."

Mr. Darcy's jaw tightened, and he stared at his cousin with unwavering resolve. "I am aware of the consequences, Richard, but I will not sacrifice my happiness for the sake of appearances. Elizabeth is the woman I love, and I will not abandon her to the whims of society. I fully intend to make her my wife and face any challenges that come our way."

The two men faced each other, the tension between them palpable. Colonel Fitzwilliam's expression shifted from exasperation to surprise at his cousin's revelation. "You plan to marry her?" he asked, a glimmer of hope in his eyes.

"Yes," Mr. Darcy affirmed, his voice steady and determined. "It is the only honorable course of action, and I am committed to our future together."

Colonel Fitzwilliam, realizing that their argument had reached a resolution, sighed heavily and stepped away. "I have said my piece, Fitzwilliam," he said, his voice strained. "I hope that you will at least consider my words. If you truly intend to marry Miss Bennet, then I will support your decision and wish you both the best."

As he left the room, Elizabeth, who had been waiting anxiously outside, entered. Her eyes met Mr. Darcy's, and she could see the turmoil in his gaze. "Fitzwilliam," she whispered, approaching him with concern. "What has happened between you and your cousin?"

Mr. Darcy took a deep breath and pulled her gently into his arms. "He disapproves of the circumstances under which our love has grown, Elizabeth. He believes that our behavior could bring scandal upon us both."

Elizabeth's eyes filled with tears, and she clung to him. "I cannot bear to be the cause of strife between you and your family, Fitzwilliam. We should have been more careful, and now it seems we must marry quickly to avoid further scandal."

Mr. Darcy nodded solemnly, his arms tightening around her. "It is true that our situation is far from ideal, and marrying hastily will undoubtedly raise eyebrows. But I will not give you up, Elizabeth. Our love is worth fighting for, and I will do whatever it takes to protect you and our happiness."

As they stood there, wrapped in each other's arms, they felt the weight of the world pressing down upon them. Yet, in each other's embrace, they found solace and strength, their love a beacon of hope amidst society's disapproval. They knew that their journey ahead would be filled with challenges, but they were determined to face them together, united by their love and commitment to one another.

As the day progressed, Elizabeth and Mr. Darcy sought moments of privacy and solace in each other's company. Whenever propriety allowed, they would steal away to a quiet corner of the orangery, music room, library, or any place where they could be alone.

There, amidst gentle laughter and blushing cheeks, they allowed themselves to revel in the heady passion that had sprung up between them.

Mr. Darcy was all-consuming, his lips fervent and his hands possessive as they explored Elizabeth's curves. The sensation of his fingers tracing her skin sent shivers down her spine, and her knees grew weak as he pressed her against the wall. In the midst of their desire, they lost themselves in each other, their hearts beating as one.

CHAPTER 6

After the evening meal, they strolled through the dimly lit halls to the music room, their footsteps echoing off the marble floors. In the quiet moments that followed, Elizabeth found herself nestled against Mr. Darcy's side, listening as he played a gentle melody on the piano. The soft notes filled the air, a testament to the passion and devotion that existed between them.

Yet, with each tender moment shared, the ever-present shadow of Colonel Fitzwilliam's disapproval loomed larger, threatening to engulf their happiness. Elizabeth sighed, nestling closer to Mr. Darcy and resting her head on his shoulder. "What are we to do, Fitzwilliam? How can we weather the storm that is sure to come?"

Mr. Darcy's arm tightened around her, and his fingers trailed down the curve of her spine, sending shivers down her back. "Together, my love. As long as we stand united, there is nothing we cannot face." His lips found her temple, kissing away the furrow marring her brow. "We knew our love would not come without trial or hardship. But it will make it all the stronger."

Elizabeth pulled back to meet his gaze. "I do not care what anyone thinks or says about us as long as I have your love. But I fear that if Colonel Fitzwilliam tells others about our intimacy before marriage, my reputation will be ruined."

"You are my family now," Mr. Darcy interrupted, his voice gentle but firm. "My love for you eclipses all else. I will do everything in my power to ensure your reputation remains intact. My cousin will come to understand that in time. But for now, I will not allow his disapproval to come between us."

His words washed away the last of her doubts and fears. Smiling, she wrapped her arms around his neck and drew him down for a searing kiss.

Mr. Darcy groaned against her lips, desire flaring as her hands slipped beneath his dressing gown to explore the contours of his body. When at last, they broke apart, he whispered, "I will follow you anywhere, Elizabeth, as long as we are together."

Tears glistened in her eyes as she gazed up at him. "As will I. No power on earth can keep us apart."

He leaned in, and she closed her eyes, savoring the feel of his lips on hers.

Suddenly, the door burst open, and Colonel Fitzwilliam stood in the doorway, his face contorted with rage. "Fitzwilliam, Miss Bennet, this has gone far enough!" he bellowed, his tone laced with disapproval.

The couple started, their hands falling away from each other as they turned to face the Colonel. Elizabeth's cheeks flushed with embarrassment, a deep blush suffusing her skin, while rage momentarily tightened Mr. Darcy's jaw.

"Must you intrude on our privacy at every opportunity?" Mr. Darcy demanded, his voice steely.

The Colonel stepped forward, his eyes flickering between them. "I will not stand idly by and watch as you ruin Miss Bennet's reputation, Darcy. You know the consequences of your actions. It is not too late to do the right thing."

Elizabeth felt a chill run down her spine as the Colonel's words sank in. Would they be forced to part ways after all they had been through?

"Richard, I have already explained to you the depth of our feelings for one another and our intention to marry," Mr. Darcy said his voice hardening. "I will not apologize for loving Elizabeth, nor will I let you dictate the course of our relationship."

"You speak of love and your impending marriage, yet you allow your passions to overrule propriety," the Colonel replied coldly. "Your reckless actions threaten everything we have built, Fitzwilliam. Our family's reputation—"

"Damn our reputation!" Mr. Darcy thundered.

Elizabeth steadied herself at his vehemence though she felt no fear. She knew the anger was not directed at her. Laying a hand on his arm, she felt the tension easing from his frame.

Mr. Darcy's eyes softened as he gazed down at her. "Our family's good name means nothing if I have not love and joy in my life. Elizabeth is my heart, Richard, and I will not give her up for the sake of propriety."

Colonel Fitzwilliam regarded them impassively, his countenance betraying no hint of relenting. "So be it. But do not ask me to stand by and watch you discard our ancestry for a hasty and ill-advised union." With that parting shot, he turned on his heel and quit the room.

Silence descended upon the room as the door clicked shut behind Colonel Fitzwilliam. Mr. Darcy paced back and forth, his frustration boiling beneath the surface. "How can he be so blind to the love we share?" he muttered, more to himself than to Elizabeth. "He values propriety and reputation above all else, even true happiness."

Elizabeth watched him with a mix of sympathy and concern. She stepped forward, gently taking his hand to halt his pacing. "Fitzwilliam, you cannot allow your cousin's disapproval to affect you so deeply. We knew not everyone would understand or approve of our love, but that does not diminish its worth."

Mr. Darcy sighed, looking into her eyes. "You are right, Elizabeth. I should not let his words trouble me so. It is simply infuriating that he cannot see past the constraints of society to the genuine love and devotion we share."

Elizabeth smiled, her fingers entwining with his. "We cannot change the opinions of others, Fitzwilliam. All we can do is continue to love and support one another. In time, perhaps Colonel Fitzwilliam will come to accept our union."

"I hope so," Mr. Darcy replied, his voice softening. "He is family, and I have always valued his friendship and counsel. But if he cannot see the truth of our love, then I will stand by you, Elizabeth, and face any disapproval the world may throw our way."

Elizabeth squeezed his hand, a determined look in her eyes. "Together, we will face whatever challenges may come. Our love is strong enough to withstand the judgment of others, and we will prove them wrong in time."

As the two lovers stood there, their hands tightly clasped, the scent of fresh lavender wafted in from the open window. The gentle sound of birds chirping in the distance mixed with the faint clinking of silverware in the dining hall below. In the quiet peace of the moment, Elizabeth could feel the warmth of Mr. Darcy's hand and the steady beat of his heart. The world may not understand their love, but they understood each other, and that was all that mattered.

Mr. Darcy held Elizabeth close as they made their way through Pemberley towards his bedchamber, his fingers gently caressing her skin. Every touch sent shivers down her spine, building anticipation with each smoldering glance.

The storm still raged outside, rain pummeling the windows of the bedchamber as Mr. Darcy drew Elizabeth into his arms.

"At last, we are alone," he murmured as he nuzzled her throat, eliciting a surge of heat that left her heart racing.

"The world fades away when I'm with you," she breathed.

"As does mine, my love," he whispered, gazing at her with adoration. "Tonight, there is only us."

Their lips met in a fiery kiss, desire pooling low in Elizabeth's belly. Mr. Darcy's hands were reverent upon her skin as he slowly undressed her. When she stood before him bare, he could only stare.

"Exquisite," he rasped. His touch ignited fires wherever it roamed, leaving a trail of simmering need in its wake.

Elizabeth flushed but held his gaze. "I am yours," she whispered. "Take me, Fitzwilliam."

A low groan escaped his lips as he laid her onto the plush velvet bedding as the rain cloaked Pemberley in the secrecy of the night.

He hovered over her, claiming her mouth in a searing kiss. "My love for you burns eternal, like the fires of Mount Olympus," he vowed.

"As does mine," she gasped, pulling him closer. "My love, my heart, my soul – they all belong to you, today and always."

Elizabeth gasped, clinging to Mr. Darcy as he filled her so exquisitely that her senses shattered into a thousand pieces. She had never known such bliss, never imagined she could feel so profoundly connected to another. He gazed down at her, his eyes dark with desire, and captured her mouth in a searing kiss.

Their lovemaking was frantic yet tender, each touch stoking flames anew until Elizabeth thought she might combust from sheer ecstasy. At last, unable to bear it any longer, a hoarse cry escaped her lips, and she arched against him. Mr. Darcy tumbled seconds after with a guttural groan, shuddering in release even as tears pricked hot behind her eyelids.

They clung to one another through the fading tremors, heartbeats slowing, souls and bodies still joined. Mr. Darcy smoothed damp curls from Elizabeth's forehead, gazing at her with open wonder.

"You have unmanned me," he whispered.

She gave a wistful smile, fingertips tracing the beloved lines of his face. "As have you, dear one."

"Tonight was..." He seemed at a loss for words, eyes gleaming. "Perfection."

"Yes," she whispered. "It was."

As Mr. Darcy tucked her beneath the bedclothes and drew her close, Elizabeth sighed in contentment. The storm may still rage, but in her heart, she had never felt more at peace.

THE NEXT DAY at Pemberley was fraught with tension and awkward silences as the unusual storm raged on. They took their meals in strained silence, his cousin still absent from the dining room.

After breakfast, as Mr. Darcy strode into the drawing room in search of Colonel Fitzwilliam, he found his cousin brooding by the window, gazing out at the relentless rain.

"Richard, have you received word from our aunt, Lady Catherine, recently?" Mr. Darcy inquired, his voice echoing through the cavernous room. "I am expecting an update on my cousin Anne's health."

The Colonel turned, his countenance darkening like the storm clouds outside. "I cannot say that I have," he bit out, his words sharp as a knife.

Mr. Darcy frowned, studying his cousin with concern. "Is something amiss?"

"Do not pretend you care for my relations when you have made it painfully clear where your true affections lie," Colonel Fitzwilliam snapped, his body tense as he took a menacing step forward. "How can you stand there, so righteous, as if you have not betrayed us all for the likes of that woman?"

Mr. Darcy's hands clenched at his sides, his heart pounding in his chest. "I will not have you disparage Elizabeth. Our love is not a betrayal."

"Love!" The Colonel spat, his face contorted with anger. "You know nothing of the concept. If you loved your family at all, you would not have embroiled us in scandal for the sake of that selfish passion."

Anger flickered in Mr. Darcy's chest like a flame, but he kept his tone level. "And if you cared for my happiness, you would not begrudge me the one thing that has brought me joy. Good day, Colonel."

"Good day to you as well, Darcy. Let us hope it remains so," the Colonel seethed, his footsteps echoing down the hall as he quit the room.

Silence descended upon the drawing room like a heavy blanket as the Colonel's angry footsteps receded down the hall. Mr. Darcy sank into a chair with a weary sigh, pinching the bridge of his nose.

Through the windows, the storm began to lessen. The roads would likely be quite impassable this day;

it seemed Elizabeth would remain unexpectedly longer at Pemberley. Mr. Darcy frowned, knowing the delay would only increase the Gardiners' anxiety for their niece.

As he watched the raindrops slide down the glass panes, Mr. Darcy couldn't help but wonder how long the storm within his own family would rage on.

"Your countenance is troubled, Fitzwilliam," Elizabeth whispered, her voice a feather-light touch upon his ear.

He spun around, surprised to find her so close, her eyes searching his with tender concern. Mr. Darcy rose abruptly. "Excuse me," he said stiffly, "I must attend to some pressing business."

With powerful strides, he left the room, the sound of his boots echoing like thunder in the silence.

Elizabeth stood there, stunned by his sudden shift in mood. She twisted the fabric of her gown between agitated fingers, feeling a knot of anxiety form in her stomach. It was clear that Colonel Fitzwilliam's opinion held great sway over Mr. Darcy. Despite his professed love for her, duty and decorum were not to be ignored.

Tears welled up in Elizabeth's eyes as she gazed into the fire, once warm and welcoming, now cold and distant. Were all of Mr. Darcy's sweet words and tender gestures just a fleeting fancy, easily discarded when the weight of responsibility bore down upon him? Had she been nothing more than a passing fancy, a dalliance to be cast aside when it no longer suited him?

The tea in her cup had long since grown cold, forgotten in the turmoil of her thoughts. With a heavy heart, Elizabeth rose from her seat and left the room, unable to bear the ache inside her any longer.

Mr. Darcy sat at his cherrywood desk, quill in hand, staring down at the meticulous notes and receipts of the sale of wool from his prized sheep. But his thoughts were elsewhere, consumed by his cousin's betrayal. They had always been the closest of companions, but now they fought over a woman. The conflict weighed heavily on Mr. Darcy, but blood was thicker than water, and he could not abandon his own kin.

A sudden knock roused him from his thoughts, and Colonel Fitzwilliam burst into the study, his eyes ablaze with excitement. "There is something peculiar brewing in the storm," he exclaimed. "You must come, Darcy."

Perplexed but intrigued, Mr. Darcy set aside his quill and rose from his seat. "What is it?" he pressed.

"Something like you've never seen before," replied Colonel Fitzwilliam enigmatically.

He gestured for Darcy to follow him, leading him up a flight of stairs and down an abandoned corridor, evading all of Mr. Darcy's questions about what could be so unusual about a mere storm. Hail? They'd all seen hail before.

Colonel Fitzwilliam held his arm out with a flourish as they arrived at the entrance to the seldom-used art room. "After you."

Curious, Mr. Darcy stepped inside the spacious chamber and walked straight to the towering windows. The evening light was dim, casting long shadows across the room. He peered out into the murky sky, trying to discern what his cousin had found so fascinating.

Suddenly, a blinding flash of pain erupted at the back of his head. Stars exploded across his vision as he crumpled to the floor, barely registering Colonel Fitzwilliam's voice echoing in his ears.

"Forgive me, Darcy. But I cannot stand by and watch you tarnish the Darcy name."

CHAPTER 7

After days of raging, the storm finally abated, revealing a clear and bright sky as Elizabeth stood in the drawing room gazing out the windows. Mr. Darcy had not returned from taking care of his sudden business. But she knew that it was time for her to return to Lambton and rejoin her aunt and uncle and reveal that she was not engaged to the wealthiest man in Derbyshire.

As Elizabeth walked through Pemberley, searching for Mr. Darcy to no avail, the silence enveloped her. The memories of their brief yet intense passion and tenderness filled her heart, and she knew they would be forever etched within it. Elizabeth had hoped that Mr. Darcy would ask for her hand in marriage, making their love a lasting commitment. He had even confessed his love for her and spoke of their being wed but had never actually asked her.

As Elizabeth continued her search, a whirlwind of thoughts and emotions swirled through her mind. She recalled Mr. Darcy's tender words and the depth of feeling she had seen in his eyes. Though he had spoken of their being wed, she couldn't help but wonder why he hadn't formally proposed. Was he having second thoughts? Or had he merely been caught up in the passion of the moment? Doubt and insecurity began to creep into her heart, dampening the joy she had felt in his arms.

But as hours slipped away, it became apparent that no such proposal would be forthcoming. She had not seen any sign of Mr. Darcy, and her heart sank as she readied her muddied clothing into a bag she found lying on her bed.

Elizabeth knew she could not leave without at least leaving a message for Mr. Darcy. She hurried to the library and found a piece of paper, penning a heartfelt note to him.

"Dearest Fitzwilliam,"

she wrote, her hand trembling as she put her feelings onto paper.

"I have searched for you throughout Pemberley, but it seems that we are destined not to meet before my departure. I must return to my aunt and uncle, who are undoubtedly worried about my prolonged absence. I tried to find you to tell you this in person, but time is no longer on my side.

Please know that I love you deeply, and my heart is filled with the memories of our time together. I will be at the Lambton Inn, awaiting your arrival. If you feel the same for me, as you have professed, I hope you will join me there and ask for my hand from my Uncle Gardiner.

Yours, with all my love,

Elizabeth."

With her note written, Elizabeth folded it carefully and sealed it with wax. Entrusting it to Mrs. Reynolds, she asked her for a carriage to be prepared, and when it was time for her to depart, Elizabeth stood in the foyer of Pemberley, her gaze lingering on all the rooms where they had shared kisses and more with Pemberley's owner. Her heart yearned for Mr. Darcy to rush down the hall, saying something about losing track of time and joining her with her aunt and uncle to ask her uncle for his permission to marry his niece. But he was still absent.

At the sound of heavy footsteps, she whirled around, her heart leaping in joy, only to be disappointed by Colonel Fitzwilliam's arrival. "Elizabeth," the colonel said coldly, "My cousin sends his apologies, but he is indisposed at the moment and unable to see you off. He asked me to convey his sincerest wishes for a safe journey."

Elizabeth's heart sank like a stone, though she struggled to maintain her composure. So he would not even see her off. After all they had shared, she did not merit even that final courtesy. She couldn't help but feel a wave of devastation wash over her as the reality of Mr. Darcy's absence settled in.

However, she kept her chin high, replying with pride, "Please convey my thanks to Mr. Darcy. Though our time together was brief, it will remain forever in my memory." Briskly, she added, "As I trust he will not soon forget me."

If her boldness offended the colonel, he did not show it. His countenance remained stony, his gaze flinty. "I shall convey your sentiment, though I doubt it shall make much difference. Good day, Miss Bennet."

He turned on his heel and strode off before she could summon a response. Tears burned behind her eyes, but Elizabeth blinked them back. She kept her shoulders straight and proud as she walked out to the carriage that would bear her away from Pemberley--and the man she had so foolishly come to care for.

The gentle breeze caressed her face, and the sweet fragrance of blooming flowers filled the air, a stark contrast to her turbulent emotions. The beauty of the countryside did little to alleviate her sense of loss and betrayal.

As the carriage pulled away from Pemberley, she felt a terrible weight upon her chest, her heart breaking with the knowledge that the man she had come to love had either changed his mind or misled her from the very beginning. She had allowed herself to be vulnerable, to open her heart to him, only to be met with cold indifference in the end. It seemed as if their passionate moments together meant nothing to him.

As the carriage rattled towards Lambton, Elizabeth felt a melancholy that settled deep in her bones. She watched the world outside with an unseeing eye, and by the time the carriage rolled up to the inn, she felt as empty as the hollow-sounding clatter of hooves on cobblestones. How could she have been so mistaken? Mr. Darcy's ardent protestations and skillful caresses had led her to believe he cared for more than a mere dalliance, yet his actions spoke far louder than his words.

She entered the bustling establishment, heading straight for the staircase up to their rooms on the upper floor. She opened the door to her room, her eyes brimming with tears, as she caught a glimpse of a figure moving in the shadows.

"Elizabeth, my dear!" cried Mrs. Gardiner, rushing forward to embrace her niece. "We were so worried about you, with the storm and your sudden disappearance! Are you well? Have you been harmed?"

"I am quite well, Aunt," Elizabeth reassured her, her voice quavering slightly. "I assure you, I have not suffered any harm during my absence." She sniffed and tried to wipe away her tears. "Did you not receive my note that I had been taken in by neighbors during the storm?"

Mr. Gardiner entered the room, his face etched with concern and deep relief. "We are relieved to have you back with us, Elizabeth. I must say I feared the worst when the storm arrived and you did not return. We stayed at the Thornhills until we could wait no longer. But we must ask, where have you been all this time?"

Elizabeth hesitated, unwilling to divulge the full truth of her stay at Pemberley. "I found refuge at a nearby estate," she said evasively. "The owners were kind enough to take me in until the storm subsided."

Mrs. Gardiner's eyes narrowed, sensing there was more to the story than her niece was revealing. "If that is the case, then we must express our gratitude to these generous individuals for their hospitality."

"Yes," agreed Elizabeth, her heart aching at the thought of Mr. Darcy. "They were truly a godsend during these trying times."

Though she tried her best to evade her aunt and uncle's inquiries, as the day wore on, it grew increasingly difficult. "Elizabeth, dear, we cannot help but wonder about the details of your stay. We would like to express our gratitude to your hosts, but you have been so reticent about their identity. Pray, will you not leave us in suspense any longer?"

Elizabeth bit her lip, staring into the crackling fire. How could she possibly tell them she had been a guest at Pemberley, and of Mr. Darcy's ardent - yet fleeting - affections? Her cheeks flamed at the mere thought.

"There is not much to tell. I stayed with a neighbor," she said, her voice barely above a whisper.

Mr. Gardiner frowned, peering at her over the top of his spectacles, his eyes taking in the dress she still wore. The quality of the fabric, the cut of the sleeves, bespoke of a lady of high station - not a mere neighbor.

"I cannot say more," Elizabeth insisted, her voice thick with desperation.

The truth would only bring her aunt and uncle pain at the loss of what could never be. Or the sadness of knowing Mr. Darcy was forced to offer for her only out of duty for having compromised her.

Mrs. Gardiner regarded her with perceptive eyes as if discerning the truth Elizabeth struggled to conceal. She tenderly grasped Elizabeth's hand. "Do not fret, dearest. We shall not press you further. But know that you can confide in us if there is ever a need."

Elizabeth whispered her gratitude. If only she could tell them of the ache in her heart, the longing for a man beyond her reach. Yet some secrets were best kept close, the bitter hidden away to spare loved ones' pain.

The Gardiners bid her goodnight, leaving Elizabeth alone before the roaring fire. She gazed into the hypnotic flames, tears slipping down her cheeks like shards of broken glass.

Mr. Darcy had given her a glimpse of heaven, only to cruelly snatch it away. The memory of his touch, his kisses, would haunt her dreams--and break her heart. She loved him with all the passion of her soul, though now she knew it could never be. The pain cut sharp and deep, more than she could have imagined.

Elizabeth wrapped her arms about herself, huddled in solitude in the firelit room, and wept hot, salty tears. As the blaze flickered and crackled, she closed her eyes, imagining the feel of his strong arms around her and the scent of his cologne mingling with the woodsmoke.

As the first light of dawn crept through the cracks in the curtains, Elizabeth finally succumbed to a fitful slumber. She dreamed of Fitzwilliam, of their love, and of a future that seemed to be slipping through her fingers like sand.

When a maid knocked at her door announcing breakfast, Elizabeth roused herself and prepared to depart the inn with a heaviness in her chest. During their breakfast, the conversation was sparse. Mr. Gardiner was anxious to return to his business after taking Elizabeth back to Longbourn. The unusual storm had delayed their departure by several days.

Anxiety gnawed at Elizabeth's stomach. As the Gardiners discussed the poor roads, she pushed her food about the plate, dread pooling in her belly. Mr. Darcy could not let her leave like this. Not after all they had shared. Not after he had declared his love to her. She could not believe he would behave in this manner.

When the carriage was called round, Elizabeth lingered behind as her aunt and uncle proceeded outside. "Lizzy, come along now," Mrs. Gardiner urged. "The storm has left the roads in disrepair, so we must set off at once."

Elizabeth swallowed hard, blinking back tears as she took a final glance around the streets of Lambton. Where was he? How could he not even come to say goodbye? The hollow ache in her chest expanded with each step as she walked to the carriage.

As they traveled out of the small Derbyshire town, Elizabeth pressed her face to the glass, straining for a last glimpse of the man she loved with all her heart. But he never appeared.

Elizabeth surreptitiously wiped her tears, her fingertips damp from unbidden sorrow. The Gardiners couldn't help but notice their niece's melancholy as they traveled further from Lambton. Her usually bright eyes were dull and distant, gazing out the carriage window at the rolling hills. Her attempts at conversation were half-hearted at best, her words trailing off into silence as she retreated into the recesses of her own mind.

Mrs. Gardiner, in particular, was concerned for her niece's well-being. "Lizzy, dear," she began gently. "Is aught amiss? You seem quite out of sorts."

Elizabeth blinked, turning to her with a wan smile. "Do not fret for me, Aunt. I am merely tired from late nights and early mornings." But her voice was raw from crying, and it sounded forced.

Her aunt studied her shrewdly. "It is not like you to seem so melancholy without cause. Did something happen during your stay to trouble you?"

"No, nothing of consequence," Elizabeth said too quickly.

She glanced away, smoothing her skirts to avoid her aunt's searching gaze. If she revealed the truth, she would face a barrage of questions she had no wish to answer. Her entanglement with Mr. Darcy was too new and fragile to subject to scrutiny.

"Lizzy." Her aunt's hand covered her own, squeezing gently. "You know you can tell me anything. I am here if you wish to unburden your heart."

Elizabeth's throat tightened at the overwhelming kindness, and she fought back the tears that threatened to spill from her eyes. How dearly she wished to unburden herself and divulge the joy and wonder of newfound love, but she dared not. This was a secret she must keep close.

"Thank you, Aunt," Elizabeth said, forcing a smile. "But there is nothing to trouble myself over."

Mrs. Gardiner observed her for a prolonged moment before giving her hand a reassuring squeeze. "I am here if you ever need anything, dear."

Mr. Gardiner, who had been listening quietly, interjected with an optimistic note. "Elizabeth, life has a way of working out, even when the path seems uncertain. Believe in yourself and trust that the future will unfold as it should."

Despite their best efforts to comfort her, Elizabeth's spirits remained low. The memories of Pemberley haunted her, and she could not help but dwell on the moments she spent with Mr. Darcy. She longed for his strong embrace and the assurance of his love, but with each passing mile, he seemed to drift further away from her grasp.

That night, in the comfort of her bed at the next stop on their journey home to Hertfordshire, Elizabeth lay awake for hours, emotions churning within her. She could not understand why Mr. Darcy had acted so cruelly. After confessing his love and sharing such tender intimacy, how could he have dismissed her so easily? Was it resentment over her former refusal of his proposal or wounded pride that led him to punish her by casting her aside like a mere mistress?

No, that was not the man she had grown to love. There had been too much genuine feeling in his embrace, too much truth in his kisses. He loved her, of that she was certain.

But then, why did he let her go? Why did he not propose again and plead with her to stay? It made no sense. Her heart was shattered, her hopes in tatters. She loved him with everything she was, only to be tossed away like garbage.

As the sun peeked over the horizon, her tears finally dried, replaced by resignation, settling into the dull ache in her chest. She might never comprehend why he had hurt her so, but she knew then that she must forget him. Even as the remaining shards of her heart broke and fell, joining the ruin of what might have been. It was the only way she could survive with any dignity left intact. It was time to leave her love for lost.

As the carriage rumbled further away from Derbyshire, drawing closer to Longbourn and the life she had once known, Elizabeth's heart grew heavier. She knew that the solace and compassion of her family would soothe her wounded soul. But she also knew that they could not heal the rift in her heart that had been torn apart by Mr. Darcy.

The Gardiners' carriage had barely crossed the borders of Hertfordshire when they were startled by the sound of galloping hooves and the rattling of a carriage approaching rapidly from behind.

CHAPTER 8

Two days prior...

The tempest had raged for days. Lightning flashed, and thunder roared, but now, pale sunlight filtered through the windows of Pemberley. Yet, Mr. Darcy remained absent. Mrs. Reynolds' heart raced with anxiety; she was accustomed to Mr. Darcy losing himself in his work, but the last few days, he had lost himself in the woman that had been lost in the storm.

The unease churned inside her stomach as she thought about their behavior during the storm. She had never known Mr. Darcy to treat anyone so callously, no matter how improper their actions may have been, especially not a woman whom she would have sworn he loved.

Mrs. Reynolds searched the estate, her concern growing more palpable by the moment. She turned her attention to Colonel Fitzwilliam once again, her voice shaking. "Colonel, I must insist on knowing the whereabouts of Mr. Darcy. It is not like him to disappear without notice, and as the housekeeper, I am responsible for the welfare of all within Pemberley."

Colonel Fitzwilliam evasively replied, trying to maintain his composure, "I understand your concerns, Mrs. Reynolds, but I assure you, my cousin is quite well. He is simply... occupied with a pressing matter."

Mrs. Reynolds's brow furrowed, unsatisfied with his response. "Forgive me, Colonel, but I cannot let this matter rest without proper confirmation. Mr. Darcy's well-being is of the utmost importance to me, and I cannot ignore my responsibilities."

Seeing the determination in her eyes, Colonel Fitzwilliam relented with a sigh. "Very well, Mrs. Reynolds. I understand your concerns, and I commend your dedication to Mr. Darcy's welfare, but he was inspecting the storm damage the last I saw him."

With a nod of gratitude, Mrs. Reynolds turned and hurried down to the waiting staff. Mr. Darcy's cousin must have thought her a fool if he believed that the master would not send his steward to inspect the storm damage.

Reaching her waiting staff, all worried, she gave quick orders in a hushed tone. "I want you to search every chamber, every corridor, and every nook and cranny of this great house. We must locate Mr. Darcy and ensure his safety." They dispersed immediately, their footsteps echoing down the grand hallways as they began their search.

It was a maid who found Mr. Darcy, at last, collapsed on the floor of the old art room. "Fetch the physician!" Mrs. Reynolds cried, hurrying to his side.

To her relief, he still breathed, although shallowly. His face was deathly pale, and a bruise marked his temple. Footmen carried him to his bedchamber while Mrs. Reynolds followed closely behind, her hands clasped tightly together, praying silently that her beloved employer was indeed unharmed and that her fears would soon be put to rest.

Poultice and cool cloths had been applied to his forehead when they arrived at his bedchamber. Though the physician could find no obvious wounds, he feared a head injury. He bled Mr. Darcy and applied leeches, urging the housekeeper to keep him warm and still. "I shall call upon him again tomorrow. Do not move him, and send word at once if his condition worsens."

With a determined nod, Mrs. Reynolds fixed her flinty gaze upon the Colonel, her eyes narrowing with contempt. "You will explain yourself. Now."

Colonel Fitzwilliam's countenance darkened, his face twisted in anger. "It was an accident. I swear it! And you have no right to question me. I am—"

"You are lying," she interrupted, her voice cold with accusation. "Leave before I summon the magistrate!"

The Colonel's eyes widened in disbelief at her words, his cheeks flushing with indignation. "I assure you, Mrs. Reynolds, I have no reason to lie. Whatever has befallen my cousin was not of my doing!"

Mrs. Reynolds remained unmoved by his protestations, her steely determination unwavering. "I have known you since you were a child, Colonel

Fitzwilliam, and I can tell when you are hiding something. I will not stand idly by while Mr. Darcy suffers!"

Summoning several footmen who had been lingering nearby, she gestured for them to take the Colonel away. With firm hands, they grasped him by the arms, leading him toward his bedchamber. The Colonel struggled briefly, his pride wounded, before relenting with a resigned sigh. "Very well, Mrs. Reynolds. I will go to my chamber, but I assure you, I am not responsible for Darcy's condition."

As the footmen escorted him away, Mrs. Reynolds' gaze followed him, her expression a mixture of anger and disappointment. She turned back to the physician, her voice trembling with worry. "Please, Dr. Harrington, do everything within your power to help Mr. Darcy. He means more to this household than words can express."

The physician nodded solemnly, offering her a reas-suring smile. "I will do all that is possible, Mrs. Reynolds. Rest assured, we will find the cause of his distress and see him restored to health."

With that promise, Mrs. Reynolds reluctantly left the room, casting one last longing look at her beloved employer before shutting the door behind her. The weight of her concern and the uncertainty of what had transpired between the cousins weighed heavily upon her as she returned to her duties, her heart heavy with foreboding.

Why had the Colonel done this? The question burned in her mind like a brand, and she vowed to uncover the truth.

As Mr. Darcy roused from slumber, the room spun wildly around him. A sharp throb pounded his skull, and he struggled to bear the feeble light that trickled through the heavy curtains. Gritting his teeth against the agony, he croaked weakly for assistance.

In a flurry of concern, Mrs. Reynolds, the ever-devoted housekeeper, rushed to his side. Her brow furrowed with worry, and she tenderly dabbed a cool cloth on his forehead. "You must rest, sir," she insisted. "Dr. Harrington bled you, but he was unsure of the cause of your distress. He shall return tomorrow to check on your condition."

"Where is Elizabeth?" Mr. Darcy rasped, his voice hoarse with pain. He tried to sit up, but a wave of dizziness forced him back onto the pillow.

Mrs. Reynolds hesitated, her heart lurching with the knowledge that Miss Bennet had departed. She suspected that Mr. Darcy had not intended for his beloved Miss Bennet to be banished and feared the consequences once he discovered the truth. But for now, she knew he needed to rest and recover.

"Miss Bennet is... resting as well," she replied evasively, dodging his searching gaze. "You should not concern yourself with anything but your own health, sir. Please, rest and regain your strength."

Mr. Darcy's eyes narrowed with suspicion, but the pain in his head prevented him from pressing further. Reluctantly, he allowed himself to drift back into an unsteady doze, his dreams filled with the image of Elizabeth's gentle smile and the warm touch of her hand.

Mrs. Reynolds sighed, watching him slumber. She knew that when Mr. Darcy uncovered his cousin's actions, there would be a bitter confrontation. But for now, she could only hope that Mr. Darcy's love for Elizabeth would prove resilient enough to weather the tempest of fury and betrayal that was surely brewing.

DESPITE THE POUNDING pain in Mr. Darcy's head, he could no longer bear the stifling confines of his bedchamber. Ignoring the waves of dizziness that assailed him, he roused himself from the bed and dressed with haste. His fingers trembled as he fastened the buttons of his waistcoat, the mere thought of Elizabeth filling him with determination to ensure her well-being.

As he stumbled through the corridors of Pemberley, a servant caught sight of him, her eyes widening with alarm. With a startled squeak, she fled down the hallway in search of Mrs. Reynolds for assistance. Unfazed, Mr. Darcy pressed on, his singular focus unwavering.

Alas, as he scoured every inch of the estate, it became increasingly clear that Elizabeth was not within its walls. Panic gripped his heart, and he staggered into the drawing room, his breath coming in short, ragged gasps.

Mrs. Reynolds, alerted by the frantic servant, hastened into the room, her expression etched with concern and dismay. "Mr. Darcy, you should not be out of bed! You are unwell!"

"Where is she?" Mr. Darcy demanded, his voice raw with emotion. "Where is Elizabeth?"

The housekeeper hesitated, her eyes filled with sorrow. "Miss Bennet...she left, sir. Yesterday, after the storm."

"Left?" Mr. Darcy repeated, his voice barely above a whisper. "Why? Who sent her away?"

"Colonel Fitzwilliam, let her go, sir," Mrs. Reynolds replied, her voice trembling. "He claimed that he acted in your best interest, but I fear his motives were not entirely pure."

A surge of fury, hotter than any fever, coursed through Mr. Darcy's veins. His hands clenched into fists at his sides, and his jaw tightened. "Where has she gone?" he demanded, his eyes blazing with anger and determination.

"Back to her family in Hertfordshire," Mrs. Reynolds answered, her voice soft but steady.

Without another word, Mr. Darcy strode from the room, his steps unsteady but resolute. He would find Elizabeth, he vowed silently, and he would confront his cousin for his duplicitous actions. Nothing, not even his own illness, would stand between him and the woman he loved.

THE CONFRONTATION between Mr. Darcy and Colonel Fitzwilliam was as swift as it was brutal. Mr. Darcy found his cousin in the billiard room, a glass of brandy in hand, attempting to appear nonchalant, but the tension in the room was thick with unspoken recriminations.

"Richard," Mr. Darcy began, his voice frigid and measured, "you have betrayed my trust and interfered in matters that were not your concern. You have no place here at Pemberley any longer."

Colonel Fitzwilliam stared back, defiance burning in his eyes. "I did what I believed to be right, Darcy. I will not apologize for it."

Mr. Darcy's jaw clenched, his fury barely contained. "Your actions were driven by selfish motives. Leave, Richard. Now."

But Colonel Fitzwilliam stood his ground, meeting Mr. Darcy's glare with an unwavering stare. "I refuse to be thrown out of your house like a common criminal, Darcy. I am your cousin, and I have known you all my life. I had reasons for my actions, even if you refuse to see them."

Mr. Darcy's expression grew colder, his tone icy. "If you do not leave willingly, Richard, I will have you forcibly removed from the premises."

Colonel Fitzwilliam's eyes blazed with anger, but he knew better than to challenge his cousin when he was in such a state. He slammed his glass onto the table, the brandy sloshing over the rim, and with a curt nod, he turned on his heel, his footsteps echoing through the empty halls as he made his way to gather his belongings.

Meanwhile, Mr. Darcy summoned the stable hands to prepare a carriage for an immediate departure. Mrs. Reynolds, having caught wind of his intentions, rushed to his side, her eyes filled with worry.

"Sir, you cannot go after Miss Bennet!" she implored. "You are still unwell, and the journey will only worsen your condition!"

Mr. Darcy remained resolute. "I must go, Mrs. Reynolds. I will not allow my cousin's deception to ruin my chance at happiness."

Seeing the determination in his eyes, Mrs. Reynolds offered a final suggestion. "At least allow Dr. Harrington to accompany you, sir. He can tend to your needs and ensure that you do not suffer any further harm."

Mr. Darcy considered her words for a moment before nodding in agreement. "Very well. Have Dr. Harrington accompany me."

With that, Mr. Darcy set about making the necessary arrangements for his journey to find his love. He would stop at nothing to find Elizabeth and mend the damage that had been wrought by his cousin's actions. Love, he knew, was worth any sacrifice.

THE GARDINERS' carriage rumbled down the narrow country road, Elizabeth's melancholy pervading the small space. Her aunt and uncle had tried in vain to lift her spirits, but the weight of her heartache was too heavy to be easily cast aside. The sound of hooves thundering against the earth suddenly filled the air, jolting Elizabeth out of her thoughts. She looked out the window, her eyes widening in alarm.

A second carriage appeared on the horizon, rapidly closing the distance between them with a fierce determination that made Elizabeth's heart race. The clamor of voices and the frenzied pounding of hooves made it seem as though the very hounds of hell were in pursuit.

"Good heavens!" cried Mrs. Gardiner, clutching her husband's arm in alarm as they saw the other carriage approaching at breakneck speed. "What can be the meaning of this?"

"Highwaymen, perhaps?" Mr. Gardiner suggested, his voice tense as he peered out the window. "But it's daylight! They never attack in broad daylight."

The sound of hooves grew louder, and Elizabeth could feel her heart pounding in her chest. As the other carriage drew nearer, Elizabeth squinted through the window, but it looked like a normal if well-appointed carriage with two drivers and outriders. Her brow furrowed in confusion as she murmured, "They must be in quite a hurry."

The Gardiners' carriage rocked violently as the other vehicle pulled up alongside them, nearly causing a disastrous collision. Mr. Gardiner gripped the door handle, his knuckles white. "By God, they're going to run us off the road!"

"Stop!" a deep voice boomed, its urgency cutting through the chaos. "Stop the carriage!"

The Gardiners and Elizabeth clung to each other as their driver pulled the horses to a sudden halt, the wheels screeching in protest. The other carriage followed suit, coming to a jarring stop mere inches from their own.

Elizabeth felt her heart racing as she exchanged incredulous glances with the Gardiners, trying to process the whirlwind of events.

Mr. Gardiner's face flushed with anger at the reckless behavior of the other driver. "I shall have words with this madman," he declared, his jaw clenched in determination.

Elizabeth tried to dissuade her uncle, her voice trembling with a mixture of fear and excitement. "Uncle, please, do not engage in a confrontation. We know not who it may be."

Mrs. Gardiner's face was a canvas of surprise and concern as she chimed in, "Indeed, my dear, we must be cautious."

As they each composed themselves, Elizabeth smoothed her skirts, took a deep breath, and felt her heart flutter wildly in her chest. She braced herself for the inevitable confrontation, her mind a tumult of questions and fears.

Mr. Gardiner, still visibly annoyed, flung open the carriage door and stepped out, his eyes fixed on the figure who had dismounted the other carriage and was now striding towards them with an air of determination.

As the man drew closer, Elizabeth gasped in surprise.

"It's Mr. Darcy!" exclaimed her aunt, who looked equally astonished.

"Mr. Darcy," Mr. Gardiner began, his voice stern, "I do not know what has possessed you to behave with such recklessness, but I demand an explanation!"

Elizabeth held her breath, waiting to see how Mr. Darcy would respond to her uncle's rebuke. She could not help but feel a flicker of hope deep within her heart.

Mr. Darcy's eyes met Elizabeth's with an intensity that seemed to pierce her very soul. She couldn't help but notice the bruise on his face, and her heart ached for him.

"You are right, and I beg your forgiveness," he said earnestly. Turning his attention back to Elizabeth, he continued, "There is a matter of great importance that I must discuss with Miss Bennet." He walked purposefully towards the open carriage door.

The Gardiners stared in disbelief, their minds struggling to comprehend the scene unfolding before them. Elizabeth, for her part, was equally dumbstruck. Her heart pounded in her chest as she locked eyes with Mr. Darcy, a thousand questions swirling in her mind.

With trembling hands, Elizabeth reached for the doorway, her breath catching in her throat as she prepared to confront the man who had captured her heart and then seemingly abandoned her. The rustle of leaves in the breeze provided calming background noise.

Kneeling gracefully on the carriage steps, he appeared entirely unbothered by the many eyes upon him. "Miss Bennet," he implored, his voice full of emotion, "I would never have let you leave, but my cousin took matters into his own hands, leaving me indisposed."

At that moment, the physician hurriedly appeared, walking briskly toward them, concern etched on his face. "Mr. Darcy, please take care! You have suffered from a severe blow to the head."

Elizabeth's heart skipped a beat as she took in Mr. Darcy's disheveled appearance and the urgency in the physician's voice. Her anger and hurt began to dissipate, replaced by a sudden rush of concern for the man she loved.

"Fitzwilliam!" she cried, her voice laced with worry. "You should not have come out here in your condition!" She moved toward him, her hand instinctively reaching out to steady him, her eyes searching his face for any sign of pain or distress.

Mr. and Mrs. Gardiner exchanged a glance, their eyebrows raised in surprise.

"Please, Elizabeth, forgive me," he implored, his eyes locked on hers, his voice strained with emotion. "I did not mean to worry you or make you doubt my intentions. I have been trying to find you ever since I regained consciousness, and I would have been by your side sooner if it were not for my cousin's interference."

Tears welled up in Elizabeth's eyes as she realized the truth behind his absence.

"Miss Bennet," he pleaded, his eyes glittering with love, "will you do me the honor of becoming my wife?"

As Elizabeth wiped away her tears, she took a deep breath, her heart pounding with a mixture of trepidation and joy. She searched Mr. Darcy's eyes for reassurance, discovering there an earnestness that touched her deeply. Her voice, though still shaky, carried the weight of her decision as she spoke, "Yes, Mr. Darcy, I will marry you."

The relief and happiness that washed over Mr. Darcy's face was unmistakable. He reached for Elizabeth's hand, his touch warm and steady. "Elizabeth, you have made me the happiest man alive. I promise you, from this day forward, I will strive to be worthy of your love and trust."

The Gardiners, who had been watching the scene unfold with a mixture of shock and amazement, exchanged glances before Mr. Gardiner cleared his throat. "Well, Mr. Darcy," he said gruffly, though not unkindly, "I suppose we ought to discuss the particulars in a more proper setting. But first, let us tend to your injuries and find a way to get all of us safely to our destination."

For a moment, Mr. Darcy hesitated as if warring with himself over some internal struggle. Then, with a decisive nod, he murmured, "To hell with propriety," and pulled Elizabeth into a searing kiss.

His lips claimed hers with a hunger that ignited her blood. Elizabeth gasped, then melted into his embrace. Startled, yet not unwilling, she responded with equal fervor, her heart swelling with love for this man who had once been her adversary but had now become her greatest ally.

She had never imagined a kiss could be so intoxicating, leaving her senses reeling. Her fingers tangled in his hair as she returned his ardor, losing herself in the sweetness of his taste and scent.

Their passionate embrace was interrupted by a discreet cough from Mr. Gardiner, a gentle reminder of the propriety they had momentarily forgotten.

With cheeks flushed and eyes sparkling, Mr. Darcy and Elizabeth pulled apart, a sheepish but unrepentant smile gracing their lips.

THE END

THANK YOU FOR READING! View Demi Monde's catalog of books.

She also writes clean and sweet Pride and Prejudice variations as Bella Breen.

If you would like to know when I release a new book, and have a secret sale just for my newsletter subscribers, sign up for my newsletter. Yes, please, sign me up!